I0531056

If Not for Love

A Highland Romance

J. Adams

II

If Not for Love

A Highland Romance

J. Adams

J. Adams

Copyright © 2014 J. Adams
Jewel of the West Publishing
All Rights Reserved
ISBN-13: 978-0615943152
ISBN-10: 0615943152

Library of Congress Control Number: 2013923527

If Not for Love

"Young Munro he took a notion
For to sail across the sea,
And he left his true love weeping,
All alone on Greenock Quay,"

- Neil Munro

J. Adams

One

Inveraray, Scotland

Another storm is rolling in. It is the kind that is bitter cold and seeps into the bones. The kind I dreaded when I was a child, poor and living in an old house with no heat, and very few blankets. Though those days have long since passed, they remain in my memory.

Since moving to Inveraray two months ago, my body is slowly acclimating to the highland weather. Of course, the Aran sweaters, wool kilted skirts, cashmere socks and boots help. I had winterized my wardrobe as soon as I arrived and I now dress like a Scot instead of a tourist. I've even acquired a slight accent, which boggles my mind. Truthfully, I have never been a tourist. That term would describe someone just visiting. I'm staying.

Shivering, I turn up the thermostat and wrap a quilt around my shoulders. Murky days like this are standard and considered another part of Scotland's wintertime beauty. Bad weather doesn't stop anyone here. This is not a land for wimps.

Gazing through the cottage window, I can see him. He is out walking again, there, just along the shore of Loch Fyne. His dark auburn hair is pulled back in a ponytail, exposing his rugged features. Puffs of fog escape his lips with each breath he takes. A heavy mist sits over the loch and thick dark clouds block the sun that had only moments ago sat in a clear blue sky. The weather in the highlands is ever-changing and unpredictable, so it is best to always be prepared–something else I've learned. How I look forward to experiencing spring and summer here.

I have watched Tavish MacLachlan walk along the loch every day for two months, and every day my writer's mind comes up with another layer to add to the Scottish highlander hero of my newest short story. Oh, the story is not really about him, but physically, he definitely fits the bill when I picture the character, owning the physique of a warrior during the times of Rob Roy and William Wallace, the kilt, Aran sweater, thick socks and *Ghillie* boots adding an earthiness to the traditional wear.

Since learning Tavish's name from a waitress in the local pub, my fascination with the man has only increased. I keep wondering what his story is. Everyone has one, and my imagination is working overtime conjuring up one for him. Glancing over at my laptop sitting on the desk near the window, my eyes roam over the latest excerpt illuminated on the screen:

Each morning, Evan McNeal walks along the shore and thinks of his lost love. She had left him without a word, taking their children with her. His heart still pines for her and he is sure it always will. She could be anywhere, for she had kin all over Scotland.

They had shared harsh, bitter words, words he

would never be able to take back. If only he could go back and relive the moments of that night. If only . . .

Pulling my eyes from the screen, I gaze down the loch a distance where he now stands, staring out over the water, his profile dulled by the mists that have thickened. A part of me suddenly doesn't like the idea of Tavish MacLachlan's heart belonging to another woman. No, I don't know him, but the thought of him longing for someone else bothers me for reasons I don't understand.

I remind myself that the story isn't really about him, he just fits the physical mold, that's all. If there is one thing we writers are good at, it's separating reality from fiction–most of the time, anyway. Totally lost in thought, I fail to notice it has started raining until the small drops transform into a heavy downpour. Peering through the rain, I spot Tavish MacLachlan. He is standing by the bench in front of my apartment.

Looking at me!

Standing with his arms folded, looking like a drowned puppy, he smiles and I smile back. He's just so adorable, and call me crazy, I open the door.

"Would you like ta come in?"

"Aye," he calls, hurrying over the gravel road. "I thank ye kindly," he says as I move aside for him to enter. I close the door, mentally chanting, *Daft is what I am I'm daft, I'm daft, I'm daft.* I look at him then. *A good daft though.*

After standing for a moment gawking at him like an idiot because my mind has gone completely blank, I come up with the brilliant comment of, "You're wet."

"Aye," he replies, a grin spreading across his face. "That, I am." He pushes back the hair plastered against his forehead as a puddle slowly forms at his feet. "Forgive me for intrudin' and making a mess o your floor."

"That's okay." My brain is finally functioning again. "I'll get you a towel." When I return from the bathroom, he slips off his sweater and I have to literally pick my chin up from off the floor as he towels off his bare chest and arms. Around six-feet-tall, his build is broad but solid, every inch of him honed muscle, his arms and legs built like tree trunks. His kilt is also soaked, but if he takes that off, I know I will have to be scraped up from the carpet. Quickly grabbing a chair from the dining table, I take his shirt and sweater and drape them over it, then place it near the heating vent to dry.

"I'll make us some chocolate."

"Thank you," he says.

I turn to the kitchen area before he can notice my flushed face. "Make yourself comfortable."

Putting a kettle of water on to boil, I pull two mugs from the cupboard and spoon in the chocolate, my mind running a mile of minute as my thoughts dwell on the fact that Tavish MacLachlan is standing in my living room, behind me! The man has no idea he has been a permanent fixture in my thoughts as of late. But now that he is here, I should get to know him.

Shouldn't I? After all, here is the hero of my story. *No, he isn't!* Now I'm mentally arguing with myself. This is not good. I can feel his eyes on me and I fight to keep from glancing back. As heat rises up my neck, I am suddenly feeling too warm in the sweater.

The kettle whistles and I pour water into the mugs, then stir before topping the chocolate with a big dollop of whipped cream.

When I finally turn, Tavish is standing by the

desk, looking at my writing awards displayed there. I'm glad the computer monitor has gone blank and he didn't see my work in progress.

"Here you go."

"Thank you," he said, accepting the mug.

"You're welcome."

He takes a sip and smiles. "It's verra kind of ye to offer me shelter for a bit. I guess I should introduce myself. I am Tavish MacLachlan."

"I'm Adia."

"I know."

"You do?"

"Aye. I asked about ye at the pub."

"Let me guess. Brandy?" She was one of the friendliest waitresses there and had been the one to tell me about Tavish.

"Aye."

"I'll confess, I knew yer name too." I am unable to keep from smiling.

"Ye did, eh? Let me guess, Brandy?"

I laugh. "I guess that's what happens in a small town."

"'Tis true. Where are ye from?"

"Originally, Black Mountain, North Carolina, but I moved here from Salt Lake City, Utah."

"In the United States, right?"

"Yes." I gesture to the sofa. "Would you like ta sit down?"

"Well, I wouldna want to dampen it. My kilt is still wet."

Grabbing another towel from the bathroom, I spread it on the sofa. "How's that?"

"Should do. Thank you."

"No problem. So have you been there? To the states, I mean?"

"No. I havena been outside of Scotland. You do a lot of traveling, eh?"

"In the states. Other than that, I've been to Sweden, Mexico and here. I have to admit though, Scotland is my favorite place so far."

"What do ye like about it?"

"Well, other than discovering one of my ancestors was Scottish, everything. The country is beautiful with all of its history, the majestic green lands and forests, and all the lochs. Waking up each morning to the view of Loch Fyne and the mountains far beyond it is wonderful. The people here are so laid back and everything moves at a slower pace. There is just something about the highlands that I feel connected to."

Standing, Tavish walks over to the window, taking in the view of Loch Fyne. "Aye, I understand. Inveraray is my home. The world is vast with many lands to explore, but I dinna think I could ever move away."

"Can't say that I blame you," I murmur, going to stand next to him where he continues to gaze at the loch.

"So, ye have Scottish blood in yer veins?"

"Not only blood, but history. My grandmother was a Calhoun. Since I'm also working on a story about her life, I researched her parent's origins and the clans ta which the slave owners whose names my ancestors were given belonged. Her father was a Calhoun, his own mother the daughter of the slave owner. My grandmother's mother was a McCullum."

"Oh, aye, Clans Colquhoun and MacCallum, though technically, you are of your grandfather's clan."

"I'm amazed at all the different spellings and

name associations."

"'Tis the same with most clans, including my own. There are over five hundred different spellings of the three names associated with Clan MacLachlan. Gilchrist and MacEwen fall in with us, Clan MacLachlan being the chief clan."

"Wow! Five hundred?"

"Aye. The phonetic spelling changes came when people married or migrated, or depending on an occupation. Some names were also changed because of illegal actions. A fugitive would adopt other names or change the spelling."

"Well, the research has been fascinating."

"Ta be sure. How long have ye been a writer?"

"For about fifteen years."

"Judging by the awards," he says, gesturing to the three crystal book-shaped trophies on the desk, "you are verra good."

"I try."

"'Tis fitting you are stayin' in this cottage. Neil Munro created some brilliant stories while living here."

"I've read some of them. He was a great writer."

We move back to the sofa and take our seats

again. "Why did ye move here? And what made you decide to make Scotland yer home?"

"It's complicated."

"I ken that. Otherwise ye wouldna have moved across the world." He leans back, resting an arm across the back of the sofa, making it impossible for my hair not to brush against his skin. His bare chest is bathed in an orangy yellow as the rain lets up and the sun peeks through the gray clouds, it's light casting a soft glow over the room. The red hair sprinkling his chest is even redder in the sunlight.

I don't know what it is about Tavish that makes me want to open up, but I do. I am about to share something I have never told anyone, not even my sisters. I have never been close to them, and my mother has been too wrapped up in her own sorrows to care about what is going on in my life. She has been that way since my father walked out on us over ten years ago. We haven't seen him since. The two close friends I did have betrayed me, so I've kept this to myself, not daring to trust anyone else.

"I was under contract with a New York publisher and I lived there in the city for three months each year. I write short stories and they published some of my anthologies. For two years, the married president of the company made sexual advances toward me that went from subtle to extremely blatant. I told him I wasn't interested from the beginning. Evidently he was used ta getting what he wanted because he wasn't taking no for an answer.

"One day he asked me to come to his office. Reluctantly I went, but I went in prepared. I had turned my phone on video to record sound and slipped it into my pocket. The man told me outright that he wanted me to sleep with him. He didn't just want me once, as if that wouldn't be bad enough, he wanted an affair. He said it would be in my best interest not ta turn him down again and reminded me that he had the power to ruin my career. After I again said no and asked him to stop propositioning me, he spouted a few choice words and told me to leave."

Tavish shakes his head. "So I assume the eejit made life verra miserable for ye after that."

I snort. "You're right, and he was an eejit. Each and every story I submitted after that was rejected. And I knew I needed ta get out and move on. Of course, I also knew he wouldn't make it easy, so I went in prepared. I demanded that he let me out of my contract and give me the rights to my stories back, not *sell* them back, but *give* them back. He laughed and told me I was crazy. However, he stopped laughing when I pulled out my phone and played the recording. Just to be safe, I'd made a copy of the recording right after I left his office the last time, and I made sure he knew this."

"Smart lass, ye are. He didna take it well, I suppose."

"Not at all. I told him that though the recording would not be admissible in court, I would make sure his wife got a copy of it."

"Ah, that was braw of ye!"

"Thanks. I got out of the contract, got my rights back and was paid the royalties owed me. Having been in the business for a while, I took what I learned and started my own little self-publishing company. I can run it from anywhere, I have total control and I make more money. So that's that."

"And ye've done it all on yer own."

"I had no choice really. What's sad is most of the employees there knew what was going on. Two of them were good friends. I wanted ta tell them, but before I could even say anything, they told me I needed to loosen up. It turned out they had both given in to the boss's demands long ago."

"'Tis a shame to have gone through such disrespect. But I'm glad ye have the opportunity to go it alone. You will be successful, I'm sure."

"I appreciate the positive thoughts, and I hope you're right."

"What kinds of stories do ye write?"

"Mainly romance, but one of my current projects is a story based on the life of my grandmother."

"She must ha been a great lady for you to write about her."

"She was. Despite her hardships, she lived an amazing life, even though she didna think she did. She died about five years ago."

"You were close to her?"

"Very."

"I'm sorry you lost her. I would love ta hear about her."

"Another time. Now tell me about you."

"There's no much to tell. I'm no married, I have

two sisters, both living in Glasgow. My mathair died when I was a wee lad. Me da lives here in Inveraray. For work, I make tartan and sell it online."

"Oooh, sounds fascinating. Where do you make it?"

"At home."

"You mean you have one of those big looms? I've seen photos of them."

"Yes, I inherited it from my grandmother. She was a tartan maker and taught me. I decided ta turn it into a business."

"She must have been talented. I guess you are too."

"I try to do good work."

"I would love ta watch you sometime."

He smiles. "I think that can be arranged. Now," he says, standing, "I thank ye for the shelter, but I'd best be off before I wear out my welcome."

I'm sad that he is leaving. "I dinna think you could ever do that."

His steady gaze causes my cheeks to warm and I feel the blood rushing to my face, making my skin turn a few shades of red. He fingers a lock of my hair, as if he has a right to.

"That's what I'm countin' on."

Two

"I don't see how anyone slept in these things."

"I dinna think they did," Tavish says, grinning at me as I try to get comfortable in the hammock stretching across one of the small cells. His blue eyes are bright, his auburn mane hanging loose, framing his rugged Scottish features.

Our tour of the *Inveraray Jail* has been quite an experience, and I mean literally. The old jail is an interactive museum where visitors can experience a little of what it was like for the inmates there long ago.

"I'm sure 'tis better than the wooden beds and

pillows they slept on for the first thirty days they were here," he adds.

"Ye're probably right," I say, attempting to get up. Tavish grabs my hand and pulls me up. "Thanks." I stretch my back. "A good masseuse would have come in handy back then."

"True," he agrees. "But they wouldna ha been used for such innocent purposes, if ye ken what I mean."

"I hear ya loud and clear. Bad idea."

"I'm no saying the sentiment wouldna ha been appreciated."

I laugh, loving his sense of humor. He is definitely full of surprises.

Like leaving my cottage yesterday with the promise of seeing me again soon, then pulling up last night with a walnut carrot cake from *Brambles*, my favorite bistro and bakery in Inveraray. He also brought cider because neither of us drink, a fact that still blows my mind. He'd stayed and we talked until late. I walked him to his car, we said goodbye, and he drove away, having made plans to take me out today. And here we are.

Today is the first time I've toured the jail since coming to Inveraray and I'm glad Tavish brought me. He has made the whole experience fun and has shared some insightful thoughts with each exhibit. Like the room where some of the old punishments can be sampled by visitors.

He turns the crank machine that males prisoners had to turn 14,400 times a day. By tightening the screw, the warden could make it harder for the prisoner to turn.

"If this was used in prisons today, I think there wouldna be so much complacency in them, no matter how well the inmates fare with the care. Of course, there would be no need for weight sets either, which would save money."

"In a quirky sort of way, you're right."

"What does quirky mean?"

"It means strange, weird. Not that you are strange or weird."

"Och, maybe I am at times, but I'm glad you don't think so."

"Not yet anyway."

He raises a brow and snorts and I laugh. "Feisty

lass."

"Oh, you have no idea."

We move on to the courtroom where over six thousand men, women and children were sentenced, some of the children guilty of nothing more serious than stealing a turnip or loaf of bread because of hunger. The jail still has the prison records. The room is set up like a circuit court in session. There are life-like figures on display and a recording of a court case is played over the speakers. We are actually listening to transcripts based on real trials held here long ago. It's a pretty incredible setup.

"That's the way I looked a few times during dull writers workshops," I say, gesturing to the figure of the tired old judge up on the bench.

"I dinna think you couldha looked that bad. That poor fellow looks like he had a run in with ole Medusa herself."

I smack a hand over my mouth, muffling a loud laugh. "Maybe he just had a bad day. Definitely had bad hair."

He laughs. "Ta be sure."

We sit for a while longer, then Tavish takes my

hand and we head to the gift shop to browse before going to grab a late lunch.

* * *

Inver Cottage-once the old castle Lachlan-is a cozy little restaurant on the shores of Lachlan Bay, Loch Fyne, and it is one of Tavish's favorite places to dine. The view is beautiful, the atmosphere is relaxing and the food is amazing. He told me the owners took the restaurant over from previous generations of MacLachlans, distant relatives of his. After dining on salmon and smoked haddock fishcakes and sticky toffee pudding, we talk over tea.

"So, explain the whole clan thing ta me. I've read a bit about it, but I would like to hear about it from the source, so to speak."

Tavish stirs his tea. "Well, I'll tell ye what I ken, but I'm no expert."

"That's okay, you're the next best thing."

He chuckles. "Since you put it that way. Well, a clan is sort of a group of kin. Most share the family names in one form or another, and each clan is recognized, identified and logged. We clans have our own tartan patterns. Most, like me own Clan

MacLachlan, have several, some of the patterns verra old. A clan's family tartan represents the district they are from and we are identified by it. Like the Clan MacLachlan district is the Argyll area, Clan Colquhoun's origin is the Loch Lomond area."

"Like the song, and the Loch Ness monster, and so forth," I interrupt with a wide smile, making him laugh.

"Aye, like tha'." He pauses, fingering a pattern on the tablecloth and I find myself mesmerized by the movement of his large hand, as well as his voice. "Many clans have a Clan Chief. The ones that dinna have a chief are called armigerous clans, which is a clan that once had a chief but have no coat of arms with marks distinguishing birth order or family position. The coat of arms is usually passed from the father ta the oldest male heir. It would identify him as chief. So basically the chief-less clan is adopted in. And no every person who bears a clan's name is a descendant of the chief. Many clansmen took the chief's surname as their own ta show solidarity, or for protection and food."

"I read a little about the Jacobite uprising and how the clanship was destroyed."

"Aye. Today it would be called 'ethnic cleansing.' The Duke of Cumberland basically had Jacobite supporters butchered. Tartan was soon banned, then the ruling was overturned."

It is such a sad history, and we take a moment to ponder all that has been shared. I finally smile, lifting my tea cup. "How grateful I am that the ban was lifted. A highlander would not be a highlander without a kilt."

He grins. "No, it wouldna be normal. No to mention I would have ta stock up on breeks, and then worry about chafing."

Coughing, I almost choke on my tea. He reaches over, patting me gently on the back and I cover my mouth with a napkin. "That–" I cough again, "really would be a worry. Of course, you would–"

"Well, hello, Tavish." The perky voice cuts me off and I look up at the flaming-haired, shapely woman.

Tavish looks up, his expression unreadable. "Molly."

"How hav' ye been?" she asks.

"Fine."

Cutting her eyes to me, she leans in toward Tavish a little. "Might I talk to ye a moment?"

"Not now."

"Please. I just got back and it's important."

As I sit listening to her, the last excerpt I added to my manuscript yesterday flashes in my mind and I mentally cringe. *Not a lost love. Please don't let her be a lost love.*

Tavish looks at me. "I'm sorry, I'll only be a moment." He gives me a half smile as he stands and I draw forth a smile in return.

As I watch them walk away with Molly's hand attached to his arm, I realize my heart is in a vulnerable position, a place it has never been before, and it is now sporting an ache I have never experienced.

I have never been a person whose head turned easily and I hold to my heart tighter than I should. I have always listened my head first, but it seems that my head, with all it's logic, is being overruled. This is definitely a first.

And I haven't the faintest idea how to handle it.

Three

When Tavish finally returns, he is alone.

"I'm sorry," he says, taking a seat again.

"It's okay." I watch him silently studying his teacup, the muscles in his jaw twitching slightly, and I can't help asking. Something inside me needs to know. "Who is she?"

"No one important."

"O-kay." His face isn't saying she is no one important. Averting my eyes, I gaze out at the loch and watch the rippling water shimmer in the sunlight, wishing for something, anything, to drive away the sadness I suddenly feel inside. There really is no excuse for it. I mean, good grief, I have only known the man for a couple of days! But I have watched him and known him in my head for a long while now.

"It's no what you think," comes his gravelly voice. "She is someone from the past who wanted ta be more to me than she was." He takes my hand and squeezes.

"You dinna owe me an explanation."

"But I do, and if there is to be anything between us, ye need ta hear it."

I sigh. "Tell me about her."

There is indecision in his eyes for a moment. Then he nods. "First, I will tell ye a little more about meself." His fingers tighten around mine. "I am a thirty-two-year-auld man who has never been in a serious relationship with anyone, which drives me sisters bonkers. My da understands me. He kens what kind of woman it would take ta move me. Until you, I hadna met such a lass."

My heart begins to melt with his words, because he puts into words exactly what I have felt for so long. I'm thirty-five and considered an old maid by acquaintances. I squeeze his fingers and he heaves what sounds like a relieved sigh.

"I met Molly when I was nineteen. She moved here from Glasgow to help her grandparents for a while. She was nice, but she wasn't for me, and though we bedded a time or two, it wasna ever more than that. For years, she made like I belonged ta her, and blethered on to others about marrying me. I finally told her one day that I didna feel that way about her and I never would. 'Twas hard to say, but I couldn't let it go on. She was angry, but she finally stopped. She left Inveraray two years ago and I hadna seen her again until today."

Though I am a little relieved by this, I can't help thinking that she is back now and things might not be over for her. Maybe she will want to pursue him again, and maybe his feelings might change. It would probably be best not to let my own feelings get involved more than they already are. I don't think I could take being hurt that way.

Something in my expression must give away my thoughts. Tavish moves his chair closer to mine and drapes an arm around the back of it. His warmth brushes against my back. "Adia, I'm no saint, but I wouldna lie to ye. What Molly wanted with me, I want with you. Her presence doesn't matter." He gently buries his fingers in my hair and I tremble at his touch. "Please believe me, lass," he says in a raspy whisper. "We can make this work. Ye're what I want."

I look into his eyes and find nothing but sincerity in them. Guiding me forward, he rests his brow against mine and I finally say, "I believe you."

* * *

As we exit the restaurant, we pass Molly, and Tavish's hand tightens around mine. He draws me closer to his side. Molly is standing just outside the door, talking with another woman. She says nothing, she simply stares, and in her eyes is a look I recognize well. I've seen it before and there are a thousand words behind it, none of them good. But just as quickly as it comes, it disappears, hidden behind the wide smile frozen in it's place.

And there is no warmth in it.

Four

We pull up in front of Tavish's home. Like most
of the cottages and buildings in Inveraray, the outside
is whitewashed Georgian. With blue shutters and trim,
it is absolutely charming.

"I love it," I say as we enter and he shows me
around. There are hardwood floors, wood counter tops
and wood trim throughout the house. The look is
totally Scottish and very cozy.

"I'm glad ye like it. My sisters helped with the
decoratin'."

"They have great taste." A woman's touch is

apparent with the colorful toss pillows on neutral-toned covered sofas. Yet the high bookcases, blue drapes and the shelf full of family photos in the living room are definitely Tavish. The place suits him.

"Is this the MacLachlan crest?" I ask, pointing to the large glass frame on the hallway wall.

"Aye."

The crest is a gold castle with three towers inside a buckled circle.

Tavish points and explains. "Each tower represents one of the three royal lines from whom the Clan Chiefs descend. They are the Dalriadic Kings of Ireland, the Celtic Kings of Scotland and the Scandinavian Kings of Hebrides. The base of the castle represents the Stone of Destiny. Upon it, the Dalriadic Kings of Ireland and Scotland were crowned."

"And what's this?" I ask, pointing to the Gaelic words beneath.

"The Clan MacLachan motto. It means strong and faithful."

"From what you've told me about yer clan history, I think that is an accurate description."

He smiles, squeezing my hand, then he takes me

upstairs and shows me the rest of the house.

"And here is the loom," he says, opening the last bedroom door.

"Wow! It's just like the ones in the photos I've seen."

"Welcome to MacLachlan Tartan Works."

The loom is an old traditional one with four foot petals and shuttles. It's strung with four colors and a tartan has already been started. Tavish explains tartan making and how each tartan has a different thread count. It is a repeat pattern that must be even. He demonstrates how to operate the loom and works on the cloth in progress.

There is something totally sexy about Tavish working the loom. Don't get me wrong, the man is sexy just *being*, but just watching the shifting muscles in his kilted thigh as he pushes the foot peddles makes me sigh. The red hairs on his calves seem to shift with each movement and I have the strangest urge to touch it. I sigh again.

Hearing my exhaled breath, he looks up and grins. "I guess I'll have ta bring ye over often to watch me work, aye?"

"Aye," I breathe. "How often do you work?"

"I usually put in seven hours five days a week."

"Do you start after your walks or do ye take a break mid shift?"

"I alternate. However, for the past couple o days, my schedule has been adjusted a wee bit."

"I'm sorry for interrupting," I playfully pout.

"I'm not. I canna think of a better reason."

I rest a hand on his shoulder and he raises it to his lips. "Thank you for bringing me over."

"Ye're welcome."

Tavish show me a few sample pieces. "These," he says holding them up, "are Clan MacLachlan tartans: Modern, dress, hunting, ancient, weathered, and the old MacLachlan pattern. You see, modern is usually strong dark colors and is plainer. Ancient, the colors are softer and lighter. Hunting has lots o green. Dress could be any of these, but it has lots of white going through it. Weathered is more faded and washed out."

"So you wear different kilts for different things."

"Aye, like a change o clothes."

"You know, I looked up the MacLachlan Clan

name meaning. It means 'the son of Lachlan,' and is derived from Lachlann, which means 'son of lochs.' But I'm sure you already knew that."

"Aye, but I'm glad ye've been learning." He touches my Colquhoun plaid skirt and examines the work. I'd had several made as soon as I got to Scotland– ordered them from Glasgow. If I had only known Tavish made tartan as well . . .

"I want ta make something for ye."

"I would love it." To wear something he created just for me would be wonderful.

* * *

Before we head back to my place, we spend a while sitting on the bench in his backyard, taking in the view of the loch below. We are quiet, each of us lost in our own thoughts. A big part of my mind is contemplating where his thoughts might be, and on whom. Is he remembering being with her? Or is he thinking about . . .

This jealousy thing is new to me and I don't like it one bit. It isn't part of who I am, or at least it wasn't before now. I need to shift my focus. At the squeeze of Tavish's hand, I turn and smile. The warmth of his adoring gaze melts my heart and all thoughts of Molly fade into the background.

For now.

Five

We spend the rest of the evening talking of everything and nothing. Tavish tells me more about his father and his sisters. Both women are married with five children between them. They are homemakers, neither of them choosing to work outside the home because there is no need. Their spouses provide well enough. His father, Neal, is retired and spends his days fishing or tinkering around the house, that is, when he is in town. He frequently leaves for extended visits with his daughters. Tavish and his father have always been very close.

"I would like ta take you to meet him."

"That would be great."

"Have to be careful, though. The man might try ta steal ye away from me."

I laugh. "I hate ta hurt his feelings, but his son has already charmed me enough to ruin it for any other man."

"Aye. I'll have to break it to him. Yer heart is already claimed. Me own has been stolen and I dinna want it back." His voice is extra gravelly, laced with the huskiness I have grown to love.

"This is true," I agree, my voice just above a whisper. I swallow hard as his gaze roams over my face, pausing at my mouth. He clears his throat and the momentary spell is broken.

"Tell me about your grandmother."

"I can do better than that." Walking over to the desk, I grab a journal from the drawer, a feeling of comfort instantly sweeping through me as I hold my grandmother's own word in my hands.

"My grandmother gave me this a year before she passed away. In it she wrote some of her thoughts and experiences." Sitting down again, Tavish draws me close. With his arm around me, I begin to read.

My name is Lizzy Baker. I was born on June 15, 1930 in Black Mountain, North Carolina. I have three sisters and one brother. William, Esther, Bessie, and Loretta. We moved to Charleston, South Carolina when I was nine and I stayed there until I turned sixteen, then I moved back to Black Mountain.

My mother, Althea Calhoun, was a good woman. She basically raised me and my siblings alone because my father was a rambler, coming and going on a regular basis. He would come home, get Mama pregnant, then leave again. Eventually, we would hear he died somewhere in Florida.

Mama cried all the time and did her best to take care of us. She made money cleaning houses.

We were left home alone a lot and did our best to take care of each other. There was little food, and sometimes there was none. The old house we lived in had no indoor plumbing and no electricity. We brought in water to bathe, used lamps for light, and heated with a fireplace, that is, when we could find wood. No one complained because this was our life and we knew nothing else.

One of the saddest things that ever happened in my childhood was losing my baby sister, Esther. My two oldest sisters moved out, so it was just Esther, William and me. We had a few friends, and since none of us went to school (no money to pay for it) we played a lot during the day. It helped to keep us from dwelling on our hunger so much. One of the boys wanted to be our blood brother, so we each cut our arms a little with a stick and pressed them together. When Esther cut herself, a small part of the stick lodged into her arm. Days later she grew sicker and sicker. Then she died. It was blood poisoning. My heart literally broke with her loss. I would write more about her, but it still hurts too much. Maybe later.

One day there was no food in the house and I was starving. I cried and prayed, then I went into the woods and killed a bird with a rock. I felt so bad for doing it, but I was so hungry, I couldn't help it. I said a prayer of thanks and another prayer for the bird, and took it into the house. Having watched Mama cook every day, I knew just what to do. I plucked the feathers off the bird, cleaned it and floured it. I put some lard in the pan, heated it up and fried it. It was good and I wasn't hungry anymore.

I stop there and close the book. Reading about my grandmother's life always makes me a little emotional and I can only handle a little at a time. I glance at Tavish to find a sheen of tears in his eyes.

"I wish I couldha known her."

"So do I. She would have liked you."

"Ye think so, eh?"

"I know so."

We sit quietly staring at one another for a moment. His eyes again roam over my face and mine do the same, taking in his dark red brows, his straight nose, the sprinkling of evening gruff on his face, and his full lips. Unable to resist, I reach up and run my fingers through his thick mane, delighting in its softness, as well as the sound of the shuddering breath that escapes him.

He touches my face, caresses my cheek. "Adia Stone, you are the most beautiful thing I have ever seen in my life."

Not knowing what to say, I swallow hard, my eyes resting on the small scar beside his mouth. Everything inside me aches to kiss that scar, and then his lips.

His expression changes then, and he draws me fully into his arms, holding me so close, his sweet breath fans my face. My heart pounding, I close the distance, lightly touching my lips to his. Something between a moan and a growl escapes him, then his mouth opens, coaxing mine to follow, his tongue sensuously delving, and every single emotion a heart can possibly hold explodes within mine.

I have been kissed before, but not like this. Tavish MacLachlan is literally making love to me with a kiss, and I am drowning in the heat generating between us. My hands get lost in his hair as one of his splays against my back then slowly roams down over my hip. I press myself tighter against him, releasing a moan of my own. He smells wonderful, a blend of soap, wool and the highlands about him, and he tastes wonderful, and I never want to let him go.

Moving his lips to my cheek, he lets them glide across my face and softly says what is in his heart. "The day you moved into this cottage is the day my life changed forever. My daily walks became something more. Just the chance ta glimpse ye in the window each day was worth everything."

I move back a little to look into his eyes, surprised. "You saw me?"

"Aye. You became my sole reason for walking by. I began to imagine what ye were thinking, wonderin' what ye thought of me. Took a storm to give me the courage ta stop."

"I'm glad you stopped," I whisper as his mouth takes mine in another impassioned kiss. I have never experienced anything as amazing as Tavish MacLachlan's kisses, and each moment in his arms makes my entire being want to fly apart at the seams and melt into him at the same time.

"I'm glad ye came to Scotland," he finally breathes against my lips. "Please dinna ever leave."

What I feel for him at this moment makes it easy to say, "I willna. I promise."

Six

Closing my eyes, I stand beneath the showerhead and let the hot water run over me, relishing the sting. My night had been filled with dreams, both sensual and hauntingly disturbing. After such an amazing late night with Tavish, all of my night visions should have been sweet, but they weren't, and I had awoken with my mind a mass of confusion. Totally weird.

The one thing that cuts through my thoughts with absolute certainty is I love that man. I love Tavish MacLachlan. It's ludicrous, right? Not so to me. I think I started loving him the first day he walked passed my cottage. I have never been in love before, which is precisely why I know what I feel is real, and there is nothing I can do about it.

But I won't tell Tavish. I can't, because he probably won't believe me. It's too soon. So, I will keep this bit of news to myself for now.

* * *

Begrudgingly, Tavish and I have decided to spend the day getting some work done, he at his loom and I at my computer. This is necessary, I know, but I already miss him so much, my heart aches. I need to take my mind off him and get my head back in the game for a while. After eating breakfast, I make a mug of hot chocolate, then taking my grandmother's journal from the drawer, I turn on the computer and begin typing in another entry.

One of the houses Mama cleaned was owned by two old white women. They were always sitting on the front porch drinking iced tea when she came. On one particular day, she arrived crying more than usual. They stopped her before she went in and asked her why she cried so much. Mama told them about her husband abandoning her and how she didn't have enough money half the time to feed her children.

They asked Mama if we were in school. She said no. She was too poor to even buy us new clothes. The two women sat Mama down and told her not to worry, they would take care of everything.

The ladies bought food and clothes for us, and paid for our schooling. We were soon bussed across town to an all black school. There was total segregation, so we never mingled outside of our race. We stayed in dorms on the campus and got an education. I never got to meet those women, but I will never forget what they did for us. And neither did Mama. She thanked God for them for the rest of her days. Mama had put pride aside because she loved us, and I vowed to do that for my future children. I would do whatever it took to care for them, and hopefully marry a good man who would not roam away from his responsibilities.

School was good and I learned as much as I could in the time I was there. All of my teachers were nice, except one. Mr. Jones was his name. I always felt uncomfortable around him because he would stare at me and make me stay after class sometimes for no reason. He would just make me stay. One day, he told me to go into the closet. He followed me in and started touching me in private places. Then he tried to rape me. I cried and begged him to stop.

I can't say anymore about that.

Closing the book, I again wipe a tear away, my heart aching all over again for the experience that happened so long ago. Though it happened to my grandmother, mentally, I relived it with her the first time I read about it, a part of me almost hating the man who has most likely been in his grave for decades. Her mother thought she was sending them somewhere safe, never imagining her daughter would have to deal with something so terrible.

Grandma was a strong woman with a story to tell, and I will tell it. Her life and her history will never be forgotten. Tom Leader, my old publisher, would never have published this book. To him, I am only as good as my romance stories. If I am not writing about lovers coming together or losing one another tragically, and one or the other finding another true love, my written words are pointless.

But writing my grandmother's story is not pointless, and now that I am discovering love with my own Scottish highlander, the other project means nothing to me.

Closing the file, I click on the other manuscript and slowly move it to the trash bin, hovering over the basket a moment, hesitating for another before throwing it away. *And that's that.*

Looking through the window, I spot Tavish walking toward the door and my heart leaps. I open it before he can knock and throw my arms around his neck.

"I'm so glad you came!"

"I had ta see you. Have ye missed me as much as I've missed ye?"

"More," I say, kissing him and pulling him inside.

"I canna stay long, I figured I would take a break for a walk, and since you're on the way . . ."

"What a coincidence. I was just taking a break too."

"Did you get much done?"

"Some."

"Working on your grandmother's book?"

"Aye."

"What about yer other project?"

"I um, decided to scrub that one for now."

"Why? Do ye do that often?"

"Sometimes. Right now my grandmother's story is more important."

Tavish smiles and caresses my cheek. "I have a confession ta make."

"Oh?"

"Aye. That first day ye let me in from the storm, when you were making the chocolate . . . well, your computer was open and I couldna help myself. I read what was on the screen."

Heat rises to my face. "Well, um . . ." I don't know what to say. And when Tavish flashes that adorable grin, I am at a complete loss.

"It was lovely, what you wrote."

"It was . . . I mean . . . wait, you liked it? You remember it?"

"Aye, I do." He slowly runs a thumb over my cheek. *"Each morning, Evan McNeal walks along the shore and thinks of his lost love. She had left him without a word, taking their children with her. His heart still pines for her and he is sure it always will. She could be anywhere, for she had kin all over Scotland.*

"They had shared harsh, bitter words, words he would never be able to take back. If only he could go back and relive the moments of that night. If only . . ."

He smiles and I cover his hand with mine, holding it against my face. "I wanted so much ta know you, to know everything about you. Your look was perfect for the hero in my story, but I couldna stand the thought of you . . . It wasn't really about you."

"I ken that, and I'm glad. 'Twould be so sad ta be him. To drive his true love away."

I can't come up with a response, so I hug him, holding him as close as I can.

"My fine bonny lass," he whispers against my ear before his lips travel to my neck. "I love ye so."

His unexpected declaration is almost staggering, but somehow, I manage to respond. "Ye're a fine man, Tavish MacLachlan, and I love you too."

"Do ye now?" He draws back a little and smiles, that familiar, mischievous light present in his blue eyes.

"I do."

"Enough ta marry me?"

I blink away the tears filling my eyes. "You really want to marry me?"

"More than ye know."

"But, we haven't known each other that long."

"I know ye well, love. And you know me, better than anyone else." He takes my face between his hands. "Ye're my heart, Adia. You've become everything to me. Now, back to my question. Do ye love me enough to marry me?"

Smiling, I wipe a tear away. "I love you more than that. Aye, I'll marry you."

"Ah, darlin'," he says, holding me close, "you have made me a happy man."

"I'm happy too. And before you go, I need ta give you something," I say, pulling him away from the window and pressing him against the wall. Clutching his shirt, I immediately capture his mouth with mine and I'm quickly locked in his arms. His kiss is heated and passion explodes between us. My lips inch to his neck and he groans, tugging my hair back and favoring me with the same, his own body shuddering at the passionate sigh that escapes me.

He takes from me another hungry kiss, then gently pushes me away. "I need to go now before I can't. If I stay, I willna be able to stop myself from desiring what is not yet mine ta have."

Smiling, I nod. "I'll see you tomorrow."

He squeezes my hand and kisses my cheek. "Tomorrow, *mo chridhe*."

I stand just outside the door a moment, waving as he walks away, admiring his perfectly-rugged kilted form, and looking forward to being with him again tomorrow. It can't come fast enough. Who would've thought I would ever have man withdrawals?

As I turn to go in, I notice a small white envelope taped to the bottom of the door. My name is written on it. I hadn't noticed it before. Closing the door, I open the envelope.

Adia,

There is something important I need to tell you. Tavish MacLachlan is not the man you think he is.

Seven

The opening words to the letter throw me off balance and I quickly sit down. Closing my eyes, I take a couple of deep breaths before continuing.

He has lied to you, just as he lied to the woman who once carried his child . . .

What?

He probably didn't tell you that, did he? There is so much you don't know.

Tavish and Molly were in love and had even talked of marriage. Then Tavish grew tired of Molly and ended the relationship. He completely broke her heart. She'd found out she was pregnant the day before and told him. He told her to abort it, and even gave her the money to do it. Tavish MacLachlan paid to murder his own bairn.

Even after all of this, Molly tried to hold on. She still loved him, you see, despite being forced to abort their child. After years of trying, begging and pleading, she finally gave up and left. Now she has come back cold and distant, but wiser. I told her you should be warned, but she refused to come to you. She didn't think you would believe her. Tavish has a way of making anyone believe anything. His a manipulator of women. This is why I took it upon myself to contact you.

So here is some advice. Get out while ye still can. Get out while your heart is still intact. Because he will break it, lass. Mark my words, he will break it and leave you a broken woman.

That's it. There is no signature.

A bout of hyperventilation seizes me and I run and grab a paper sack from the kitchen drawer and hold it over my face.

Breathe, breathe, breathe.

I can't believe it! I just can't. Yet doubt is present in spades. Things have moved so quickly between Tavish and me. Has it all been an act on his part? An act to get me into his bed and use me until he grows tired of me?

No, that's not it. He had the opportunity to take advantage of me today and he didn't. Was that an act as well?

I wipe my eyes before the tears can fall and give myself a good shake. How can I believe accusations written by a total stranger? It could have even been Molly who wrote it, in an attempt to come between us. Tavish loves me. I know he does. But how can I be sure? How can I be sure of anything?

My emotions are bouncing up and down like a yo-yo and I can't seem to rein them in. "I have to get out of here." I am not running away, just taking a short break. I need some breathing room. Tavish is too close and I need to think.

Rushing to the bedroom, I grab a bag and throw in a change of clothing and toiletries. I take a writing pad and pen from the desk, deciding to leave my computer. Checking the place and making sure everything is turned off, I throw my bag in the car and leave.

Eight

I drive until I reach the resort town of Oban and decide to stop. I check into a hotel and spa, renting a room with a view of the bay. Since moving to Scotland, I've grown so used to looking out over the loch, the watery sight has become a part of me. This town is supposed to be the seafood capital, but I don't think I could enjoy it much even if I did have an appetite.

Sitting on the edge of the bed, I ponder the letter and wonder how a day that started so amazing could change so drastically. One minute I am downing in euphoric bliss, wallowing in Tavish's love, the next, I am nursing an aching heart. My sisters have always called me a spaz. Maybe they are right. That fact does not stop the questions.

Could Tavish really be someone so cold and unfeeling? Cold enough to have his own baby aborted? Could he really be that heartless? The Tavish I know could never do such things. And yet . . . do I really know him?

My brain hurts too much to think anymore. Feeling emotionally drained, I lie on the bed and close my eyes. When I finally open them again, the sun is setting and I check the clock. 8:00. I've slept for four hours. I take a moment to freshen up, then head down to the restaurant and grab something light to eat. Afterward, I go for a short walk around the grounds, wishing Tavish were here with me. Of course, that would be defeating the purpose. I am here because I need space, though to be truthful, space is the last thing I want between us. I just need to figure this out. Then I can go back and again give him my whole heart. Truthfully, he still has it and I don't think his grip will ever loosen. I just need *me* to be okay again.

For some reason, the words of one of my favorite

poems come to mind.

       Can you hear it, love, mine soul's serenade?
Is thy heart touched by its desperate whisper?
Mine own wretched internal organ beats unceasingly,
longing for it's sweet cadence to be heard, and understood.
Do the ears of thy soul weep in open adoring emotion?
Or is all tone and feeling masked, untouched by this poor
specimen?

But lo, I see thy soul now, love, hear its shattering voice.
I feel its whispered caress against mine own skin.
The unceasing beats in complete synchronization,
exercising a longing ear pressed against heated warmth.
The intertwined trail of tears calling forth a rush of sound;
the unmistakable sound of love.

The piece was written by the Swedish poet, Dylan Thomas. He was named by his parents after the original master poet. He wrote it for the woman he loved and eventually married. I don't know why, but right now the words affect me more than they ever have. Maybe it's because when I read it before, I didn't know what being in love felt like. The words always struck me as a terrifyingly-beautiful agony, the kind of love I longed to experience but feared at the same time.

I understand now, Dylan.

* * *

Before going to bed, I read the letter again, trying to keep an open mind, but it is hard when my heart is full of fear that the bottom may be dropping from under my world. I read it again and again, each time acquiring a little more doubt of its validity. Refolding the letter, I slip to my knees by the bed and petition God to help me discern Tavish's character. When my head finally hits the pillow, I drift to sleep with the faith that things will be clearer in the morning.

* * *

This morning as I awaken, my thoughts are indeed clearer and my heart knows what it wants. It wants Tavish MacLachlan with a yearning that cannot-that will not-be denied. Until he gives me a reason to doubt him, I will choose to believe what he told me, that there was nothing more between them.

I quickly shower and dress and call Tavish. I completely forgot that he was coming to pick me up this morning. When he doesn't answer, I mentally kick myself for being so stupid. Running off like that was definitely stupid, and obviously not a mature way to handle everything. I finish getting ready, check out and get on the road.

I'm sorry, Tavish. I'll explain everything when I get there.

* * *

Tavish

Tavish repeatedly knocks on Adia's cottage door, but she doesn't answer. They had agreed to get together this morning and go out for brunch, but when he'd called and there was no answer, he decided to come over. He had missed Adia fiercely yesterday, but they had both needed a day to catch up on things. Still, he'd had to come and see her, if only for a few moments. He loves her to distraction and he had needed to tell her what was in his heart.

Molly's appearance two days ago had been unsettling. The woman hounded him for years and the two times he'd allowed her to lure him to her bed had been the biggest mistakes of his life. He had been young with overactive hormones and she was willing. He knew he shouldn't have done it and had regretted it. He even apologized to her and promised himself it would never happen again. He'd been determined to keep that promise, but Molly had other plans.

For years, Molly basically stalked Tavish, managing to show up wherever he was, declaring her love for him. But he knew it wasn't really love. He wasn't the only guy to have been the object of her affections, for there had been many. But he was the one she had been determined to have. He finally had to confront her and be brutal in his declaration that there would never be anything between them. Then one day she left. That was two years ago. Now she is back.

Drawing his thoughts to the present, Tavish knocks once more. Heaving a resigned sigh, he gets in the car and heads toward town to look for Adia.

Nine

Tavish

Tavish is worried. He has been driving around looking for Adia, checking every place they have gone together. He has walked in and out of shops, searching with no luck. She may be a grown woman, but he is still worried and he prays nothing has happened to her.

"Any luck?" Brandy asks as he enters the pub.

"None." He takes a seat at the end of the bar. It is still early enough that the lunch crowd hasn't started trickling in yet.

"I hate ta add more to yer worries, but Molly

was in here th' other day askin' about ye and Adia. I told her nothin', but she's like a dog wi' a bone. Finally had ta ignore her."

"I'm sorry, Brandy. She tracked me down at the Cottage that day, askin' ta talk to me. I gave her a moment and she blethered on about how she missed me and came back ta work things out."

"There was never anythin' ta work out."

"Something that we all know." Tavish shakes his head. "I dinna understand it. She's been gone all this time, then out of nowhere she shows up starting the same auld game again."

"I'll don' think ye'll ever understand her, sae don even try. There's no rhyme or reason ta what she does. I'll do what I can ta steer ye clear of her."

"I thank ye."

"Can I get ye anythin'?"

"No, I'm going to head back to my place, maybe stop by Adia's again on the way."

"Dinna worry, she'll show up soon."

Tavish gives her a half smile of thanks and leaves. He stops by Adia's again, hoping to find her there, but his hope is in vain. Swallowing his frustration, he heads home.

* * *

When Tavish turns into his driveway, he spots an unfamiliar car. He pulls up next to it, sees the red curls and swears. Would he never be free of this woman?

"What do you want, Molly?" he asks, getting out. There is no kindness in his voice or expression. The time for civility has passed.

"I just want ta talk to ye."

"I have nothing ta say to ye, and there is nothing you can say that I want ta hear."

"She's not good enough for ye. That woman ye're seein'."

"You dinna know anything about her."

"I know she's some pitiful American writer who latched onto the first available Scot she saw."

"How did you . . ." Closing his eyes, Tavish takes a deep breath and counts to ten, swallowing his anger. "Get off me property, Molly," he says, his voice chilly but controlled. "Dinna come back. Stay away from me, and stay away from Adia."

"You don't mean that," she says, grabbing his

arm as he starts up the front porch steps.

"Aye, I do. Go back ta where ye came from and leave us be."

"No, I won't," she says. Then grabbing his head, she presses her lips to his."

Disgusted, Tavish shoves her away, but not before turning to see the shocked look on Adia's face as she pulls up.

Ten

I'm going to be sick.

Excited and anxious to see Tavish to apologize for standing him up this morning, I had rushed over to his place without even stopping by mine. I knew he was probably worried.

Boy, was I mistaken!

The last thing I expected was to pull into his driveway and find him with her. Kissing her! My insides scream at the sight of them together. It is more than I can stand.

"Adia, wait!" Tavish yells.

I back out as quickly as I can, pulling away just as Tavish reaches for the door.

Tears blur my vision as I drive back and I futilely wipe them away. I ask myself over and over how this could have happened. How could he do this to me? To us? I had made up my mind to trust him and this is what I get. Now I am so lost, I don't know what to do. One thing is for sure. I'm done crying. I will waste no more tears over him.

Driving through the city, I glimpse the holiday decorations through my blurred vision. Lighted holly and garland dress the windows, adding a charming festive look to the white-washed buildings. For a change, I thought I would finally be spending a Christmas with someone. Looks like I will be alone same as always.

As I reach the cottage, Tavish pulls up behind me. He must have been doing some major speeding to catch me. Running into the house, I try to slam the door, but his arm quickly snakes through and pushes it open. Having no desire to talk to him now–or ever–I rush to the bedroom, but he is a lot quicker than I am and grabs the door handle before I can push it shut.

"Damn it, Adia, talk to me!"

"Why? There's no point! There's nothing else ta say."

"Oh, I've got plenty ta say, woman, and you will hear it!"

He takes my arms in his hands, his grip tight and solid. Squeezing my eyes shut, I look away, fighting the tears with all I've got, but I quickly lose the battle and scoff in anger at the wetness tracking my face. I finally raise my eyes to his, resigned to defeat, attempting to steel myself to the softening of his beloved features. His grip loosens, his large hands caressing. The goosebumps on my skin are a betrayal to my war-torn heart.

"I wasna with her. She came ta me. I was trying to get her to leave."

"You kissed her." The memory of the two of them together is seared in my mind. His kisses were supposed to be mine, not hers!

"She kissed me, an act that was most unwelcome."

"It doesna matter anyway. I don't know why I am even still here, or why I came in the first place. Who in their right mind just drops everything and moves to a foreign country?"

"I'll tell you why ye're here." His hands tighten on my arms again. "You're here because you are mine. Do you hear me? Ye're mine."

"But she will never let you go."

"How many times do I hav' ta tell ye? I wasna ever hers. There was never anything between us, and there never will be."

"You kissed her, Tavish."

"I told you, she kissed me. I want nothing ta do with her. Why will you no believe me? Why do ye doubt my love for you?"

"Because of this," I say, throwing the letter at him.

He catches the envelope and removes the folded paper. "What is this . . ."

I silently watch him read the letter, his expression morphing through various emotions: shock, disbelief, anger, sadness, and finally, resignation.

He looks at me. "It's not true. None of it is true." He sighs, his eyes weary. "You have ta believe me. I couldna do such a thing. No woman deserves that kind o treatment, even her. But she is lying."

"I believe you," I finally say. And I do. Deep down I know he is telling the truth. The redhead has been a thorn in my side from the moment she walked into *Inver Cottage*, staking her claim to him and doing everything in her power to oust me from his life. She has a history with him. It may not have been in the romantic way she claims, but they have a history just the same. All I have is the last week. How do I compete?

"I don't know if I can do this. I'm thinking about going back to the states for a bit, just ta–"

"No!" He again takes my arms in his hands, shaking me a little, his face a mask of mixed emotions, his blue eyes fixed on mine. "You canna run away from this, from me."

Pulling away, I slip by him and move to the living room window and stare out at the loch, tears again trailing down my cheeks. I love this man more than I ever imagined loving someone. He is the first man I've ever given my heart to. Now I just don't know what to think.

"I dinna know, Tavish," I murmur. "The women

in my family have always been unlucky in love. Maybe it will always be that way. The Stone family curse." Resting my forehead against the window, I feel his warmth before he even touches me.

"The day I stood outside your cottage in the rain and you smiled at me, I knew I wouldna ever walk the loch again without yer smile in my mind." He gently turns me, taking me in his arms, his love lying naked before me in his eyes. The tears in them are my undoing. "I belong ta ye, *mo ghraidh*. You're in in my verra soul. Sometimes I wake in the night lonesome and aching for ye, wishing you were lying next to me, wanting ta take ye into myself. When we're together and my arms are about ye and yer mouth is beneath mine, it's all I can do not ta crush ye and keep you locked against me forever. Each time I kiss you, I want ta take your verra breath and give ye mine. No woman has ever had such a claim on me, and no one else ever will."

He gently cups my cheek. "I love you, Adia. And if I have ta follow ye from Scotland to prove it, I will. I've never left these shores, but I would leave with you. If not for any reason but love, I would follow." He wraps a hand in my hair and cups my scalp, his other arm holding me against him. "I willna lose you. I can't, because it would be the death o me."

Releasing me a moment, he reaches into his pocket and pulls out a ring, then promptly slips it on my finger. The ring is beautiful, a canary solitaire set on a white gold band surrounded by tiny diamonds. "I bought this for ye last night, just before Shemus locked up his shop." Drawing me against him again, he breathes again my cheek, "Marry me soon, *mo chridhe. Mo ghraidh.*"

Wrapping my arms around his waist, I surrender my mouth to his.

I don't know what I will do, but I know I can never leave him. Never. I don't have the strength.

Eleven

Two months later.

Hitting the button to shut off the alarm, I attempt to get up, but a muscular arm tightens around me and I am unable to move.

"Stay just a wee longer, love." Tavish's gravelly voice is raspy with sleep.

"There is a lot ta do before your da comes, *mo dhuine.*"

"We have time," he growls, kissing my neck, sliding a hand over my hip.

"But I need to . . ." His mouth is warm on my

skin. "Whatever you say," I concede with a sigh, and we are quickly lost in each other.

Tavish and I were married exactly two months ago today. We actually tied the knot a week after he gave me the ring. Standing on the shore of Loch Fyne with his whole family present, we took our vows, pledging to love each other forever. I wore a white vintage Celtic gown with an empire waist, embroidered with gold Celtic knot work. Tavish was dressed in a traditional wedding kilt, the jacket and waist coat fitting him beautifully. Though I was cold, the coordinating woolen white sweater I wore and our love kept me warm.

A few days later, I had a simple announcement made and sent one to my mother and two sisters. They never responded, most likely upset that I hadn't invited them, but that was okay. It's not likely that they would have come anyway. And Tavish is all the family I need. Besides, I'm sure we will get to the states one day and they can meet him then, if they choose to make the effort.

Neal MacLachlan is now the other man in my life. I felt a kinship with him the moment we met.

Standing a couple of inches shorter than his son, sharing the same build and auburn hair, Neal has a stern, commanding presence. That is, until he smiles. Then he turns into a Scottish teddy bear and you just want to hug him. Christmas was seven weeks ago, and because Neal has been with his daughters' families in Glasgow all this time, we decided to make a Christmas dinner and share it with him. I've been excited to try my hand at some of the Scottish dishes.

"I love you," I say a long languorous while later.

"And I love you, my verra fine wife."

"Should we get up now?"

"I suppose so. But dinna stray too far today, for my need for ye hasna been completely quenched."

Smiling, I run a hand over his chest and kiss him again. "I don' think either of us will ever be quenched, but I'm sure I can find a moment later ta see to that."

* * *

Molly

Molly Kirkpatrick has a job to do, but nothing has gone the way it was supposed to. Her objective was simple enough and the execution had gone well, but the outcome had not. The letter Molly wrote had done its job. It had caused a rift between Tavish and Adia, a result that should have been permanent. Then she'd glanced Adia coming around the corner and a bonus opportunity had presented itself. The kiss should have definitely been the end of it, but not only did the relationship last, Tavish actually married the woman.

Well, there is nothing she can do about that, but all is not lost. She has one more trick up her sleeve.

Molly hadn't wanted to do this. She'd never planned to step foot in Inveraray again. Her parents are settled in London, her grandparents moved to Glasgow, and until now, there has never been a reason for her to return. She'd even put another possible relationship on hold for this. Molly knows she is attractive and there has never been a shortage of suitors. For the past year she has been stuck in a one-way relationship that she thought was going somewhere. It didn't, and this is the result. She has always made a fool of herself when it comes to men, always desperate for love, not wanting to be alone, and she has frequently looked for love in the wrong places. Then when she has found it, she pushes it aside for something more. What a fool she is, and has been all her life. She let so many opportunities pass her by.

How did she get here? Of course she knows how, but she pushes the answer away. Giving herself a mental shake, she puts her thoughts in order and plots her next move. She has grown tired and this time it has to work.

Slipping a clean blouse over her damp hair, she casts her eyes around the cozy room. The Inveraray Hotel has always been one of her favorite places, but staying here has gotten old and she longs to get back to the small apartment that had become her sanctuary years ago. She is ready to be done.

As she opens the door to leave, her cell phone rings.

"Hello."

"Is it done?"

"I'm working on it."

"No need for me to remind you what is at stake."

"No, Ben, there is no need."

Hanging up, she sighs. There is a lot riding on this and nothing is going to stop her from finishing what she started.

Twelve

"How's my lass?" Neal hugs me and kisses my cheek.

"I'm good. How are you?"

"Well, I'm here with ye, so it's a bonnie day!"

"Stop trying ta steal me wife, da, and get your own."

"I jus' may hav' ta." He closes his eyes, sniffing the air. "Somethin' smells verra good."

"I hope it tastes as good," I say. "I followed the directions to all the recipes exactly."

Neal laughs. "I'm sure 'twill be grand."

"How was your trip?" Tavish asks.

"'Twas good ta spend time with the wee ones again, but it took a lot out o me this time. Glad ta be back."

"We're glad to have you back," I tell him. "And I'm sure yer appetite is intact."

"Och, to be sure. But before we eat," he adds, sitting down, "will ye share a little more about yer grandmother?"

I smile and nod. Tavish's father had been fascinated the first time I shared bits of Grandma's life with him. He said that though he didn't know her, he felt a kinship with her just the same.

"I'll get the journal for ye," Tavish offers. "It's in yer office, right?"

"Aye, thanks." When we married and Tavish's home became mine, he decided that I needed my own place to write since he has a room for his work. He bought a desk, a chair and a bookcase and turned one of the spare rooms into an office for me. I then decorated it with photos, plants and large colorful cushions, transferring it into a writing haven. Since it is next to our bedroom, I have a perfect view of the loch. I asked Tavish why he hadn't chosen the room for his tartan making. He said he preferred to work facing the front of the house. That way he could keep an eye out for coming visitors and customers.

Tavish hands me the book and sits close to me. I grin at the eagerness in the eyes of the two men. They are like children waiting to hear a bedtime story.

When I was sixteen, I moved back to Black Mountain. My oldest sister had moved back the year before and lived in her own apartment. I stayed with her for a while. I missed Mama, but it sure was nice being out on my own.

It was about this time that I met the man I would spend the rest of my life with. Milton Stone had just gotten out of the army when we met on the train. He was a good-looking man. Tall with toffee-colored skin, curly hair and a gold tooth that winked at you when he smiled, he was the quite the catch and caught many female eyes wherever he went. But I was the one he picked. And I was no slouch myself.

I had barely turned seventeen when we were married, and a year later our first daughter was born. Six more pregnancies quickly followed, but only three produced children, two more girls and a boy. The children provided us with a lot of laughter and many tears. It was a hard life, made even harder when Milton began drinking. I loved the man to death, but he became volatile when he drank and he hit me quite few times until I put my foot down. I finally told him one day it was me or the bottle. I was done being a punching bag. He knew I was serious, so he gave it up.

I'm not saying everything was rosy after that. We still had our trials, but life was better and we took on everything together.

"I don't know how she did it," I murmur. I don't know if I could forgive a man for hitting me, and I promised myself a long time ago that when–or if–I ever got married, if he hit me one time, I would not be around long enough to give him a second chance because there is always a second time, no matter how much they promise otherwise.

Looking into Tavish's eyes, so full of love, I know with absolute certainty he will never hurt me. He couldn't without hurting himself. I know him well enough to know this. I read a little more.

Miss Hunt was a great lady. I cleaned her house

for twenty-five years. She never married and had no family. I was deeply saddened when she died and I still miss her to this day, because she never treated me like an employee, she treated me like a friend. In her will she left me fifty thousand dollars. We used it to pay off the house and remodel. Goodness knows the old place needed it. Because I was tired of white walls, I had every room painted a different color. When the workers finished, it was a beautiful home, and I planned to live the rest of my life there. I could never have guessed my life there would be so short.

Mama did eventually move in with us. It was on her seventieth birthday. Ten years later she died in her sleep. Losing her, and then Milton five years later, were two of the hardest things I've ever had to face. Suddenly I was alone. I hadn't been alone since I was sixteen. Getting old had never seemed so hard.

But one day I finally stared mortality in the face. I accepted it, and I moved on.

Sighing, I close the book.

"A strong lass, yer grandmother was," Neal says.

"I wish I had her strength."

"Ye do, *mo chridhe*," Tavish whispers against my brow, his lips caressing in a way that makes me kind of wish we were alone.

"My Mary was a strong woman." Neal's expression is one of remembering.

"You must still miss her."

"Aye. Always. No finer woman roamed this earth. But I'm sure my boy here feels the same about ye."

"Oh, aye," Tavish agrees. "I'm a verra blessed man."

I smile at him and then his father. "Well, shall we eat?"

"Ye dinna have ta twist my arm," Neal says, quickly making a beeline to the kitchen table and we laugh.

Tavish says, "We MacLachlans pride ourselves on our instant appetites."

"Don't I know it." He chuckles, wrapping an arm around my waist as we follow Neal.

"Ah, would ye look at that!" Neal says as I uncover the dishes.

"I did a lot of this last night. Tavish helped."

Our meal consists of roasted turkey, potatoes and parsnips, stuffing with sausage meat, sage, onions and chestnuts. Bacon rolls (a Scottish roll with bacon) kilted chipolata sausages (sausages wrapped in bacon) Brussels sprouts, carrots, peas, red wine gravy, bread sauce, and cranberry sauce. And for dessert, Christmas pudding, cloutie dumpling, and Scotch trifle.

Tavish blesses the food and we dig right in. I'm amazed at how great everything tastes. I've never had many of the dishes, but I am sure they will now be some of my favorites. Neal praises the meal, telling me it is just as good as his wife's cooking. I thank him for the amazing compliment.

"So what about the Christmas story ye wrote?" Neal asks. "Tavish said 'tis a good one."

"Would ye like ta hear it?"

"Aye."

Tavish takes down the copy I have hanging on the side of the refrigerator.

"Are you ready?" I ask, swallowing a bite of sausage.

Both men nod, their cheeks full and I laugh.

"Okay, here we go."

Once upon a time, there was a kind and very lonely old man who lived in a small cabin in the woods. His home was secluded from the rest of the village, but this was not by choice. For years, he was afflicted with a skin ailment. He had sores and scabs all over his face. Because the people in the village thought the condition was contagious, they sent him into the woods. He kept his face covered with a mask whenever he went out, even though there was no one around to see him.

Though this was a trial for him, the man was grateful to have a home. He had a greenhouse that he built himself and grew his own vegetables all year. He also had a good aim with the bow and could get meat whenever he needed it, so he never went hungry. He had everything he needed–but he was still lonely.

It was Christmas Eve and the old man went out to collect wood for the week. A storm was about to blow in, guaranteeing the small village a white holiday. Walking along the edge of the woods, he spotted something lying amidst the trees. Moving closer, he saw that it was a man.

The old man stooped down and turned him over. The face was bruised and battered, but beneath the bruises, he could see the man was young.

Using what little strength he had, the old man lifted him and carried him to the wagon he used to collect wood. He draped the young man over the wood, tied the rope around himself and pulled the wagon back to his home.

When her got there, he carried the young man inside and laid him on his own bed. He cleaned the bruises on the young man's face and cleaned and bandaged the gash on his head. Covering him with a blanket, he sat in a rocking chair in the corner and watched him sleep.

When the young man woke a few hours later, the old man fed him some soup.

"Where am I?" the young man asked as the old man helped him lay back down.

"You're at my home in the woods. I found you just outside the forest. What is your name?"

"I don't know," the young man answered. "I can't remember."

"Do you remember where you lived or came from?"

"No." The young man began to cry. "I'm sorry."

"It's okay. Everything will be all right. You can stay here. It is Christmas Eve after all. You can't be *without a home at Christmas."*

The young man wiped his face, wincing as he touched the sore spots. "Thank you."

"You're welcome. Tell you what. Since you can't remember your name, we'll just call you Joseph for now, okay?"

"All right."

"My name is John."

"Thank you for taking me in, John."

"I'm happy to help."

Joseph looked up at John. "Why do you wear a mask?"

John touched the leather covering his face. "Because I was afflicted a few years ago with a skin condition. Because the people in the village were afraid that I was contagious and didn't wanted me there, I live here in the woods."

"You have no family?"

John shook his head, his eyes sad. "Not anymore."

"How sad for you, and how lonely."

"It's all right." John smiled. "I am blessed with everything I need. And you are here to share this Christmas with me."

Joseph smiled back. *"Then it is I who am blessed."*

* * *

Later that evening after Joseph gained some of his strength back, the two men sat in the small front room and sipped hot chocolate. They absently gazed at the humble little Christmas tree, each lost in his own thoughts.

"I wish I could remember who I am," Joseph said.

"So do I," John agreed. "Somewhere, you have a family that is missing you. But I can't help being thankful that you are here. It has been a long time since I had anyone to talk to. In fact, you are the first person to ever be in my home."

"You said you had family. What happened?"

"Well, my wife died giving birth to my son. He is gone now, too."

"You mean he died?"

"Truthfully, I don't know. He left seven years ago when he was fourteen. I haven't seen him since."

Joseph looked puzzled. "Why would he leave? How could he just abandon you that way?"

"He said there was nothing for him in the village and he wanted to travel and see the world. So he *packed a bag and left."*

Joseph shook his head. *"What a selfish thing to do. I could never do that to my father. I don't remember either of my parents, but if my father is like you, I will count myself blessed when I do remember."*

John smiled. *"And he is blessed to have you."* He looked at the bruises on the young man's face. *"You look like you ran into some trouble. You sure you can't remember anything?"*

"I wish I could, but part of me is scared to remember. What if I was like your son, selfish and thinking of no one but myself? I would be so ashamed. Maybe my parents don't even care where I am."

"Any parent who truly loves their child unconditionally will want that child back, regardless of what drove them apart." John paused, staring into the fireplace. *"I would give anything to have my son back. I would tell him how much I loved him and that nothing else mattered."*

"When I finally get my memory back, I will return to my family and tell them how sorry I am for whatever I've done."

"Then trust that God will get you back to where

you belong."

The evening grew late and the two men decided to turn in. Joseph told John he would take the extra cot, but Joseph insisted that the young man take his bed since he still wasn't well. John wanted him to be comfortable.

After making sure Joseph was settled for the night, John took a pillow and a couple of quilts from the cedar chest, and settled himself on the cot. He removed his mask and lay back on the pillow. Turning to his side, he stared into the fire as tears blurred his vision. As he closed his eyes to sleep, he heard a voice whisper the words he'd spoken to Joseph earlier.

"I would give anything to have my son back."

As he drifted off, that same voice whispered, "As you have given of yourself, so shall you receive."

* * *

When John woke the next morning, he reached for his mask, but it wasn't there. Not wanting Joseph to see him, he ran to the bathing room to grab his extra mask. Seeing himself in the mirror, he touched his face, releasing a soft cry. Tears streamed down his cheeks as he gazed at his reflection.

His face was perfect, his skin soft and unmarred by the sores and scabs that had covered it for so many years. Dropping to his knees, he thanked God for taking the condition away. Startled by the sound of Joseph's voice, he looked up.

"I remember now."

With those three words, the young man's countenance changed before John's eyes and he gasped.

Dropping to his knees, Joseph touched John's face as tears streamed down his own. "I'm so sorry."

John pulled him into his arms and held him, then drew back and kissed his cheek.

"My Joseph. My son, welcome home."

"Ah, Adia, that's a beauty!" Tavish says. "Ye're a gifted lass."

"Thank you." I am warmed by his praise.

"I'll have ta read yer other stories."

"Well, hopefully you will enjoy them."

"Och, ta be sure."

We eat until we are completely stuffed, then we eat a little more. By the time we are done, we're all moaning and groaning and in need of a nap. Tavish and Neal fall asleep in the living room recliners while watching television and I head up to our room to take a nap, mentally patting myself on the back, happy that the meal turned out so well.

Somewhere in my dreams I hear arguing, and it feels like I have only just fallen asleep when Tavish wakes me. Groggily taking in the grim look on his face, I am instantly awake.

"What is it?"

"There is someone here ta see you."

I ask who, unprepared to hear the name he practically spits out.

"Molly."

Thirteen

For a moment, I watch Molly where she stands on the front porch, pulling the coat tighter around her. She definitely does not dress like a highlander, her clothes suited more for the big city. Wherever she has been living for the last two years, I don't think it has been Scotland. In fact, she dresses like someone from the states. Only her accent gives her true origin away.

"What do you want?"

"I wanted ta apologize for what I did. I'm really ashamed of the way I have been. I'm so sorry for lying, and for tryin' ta make you believe there was something more between Tavish and me. There is no excuse, and I don't expect you to forgive me or even pretend to, but I just needed ta tell ye."

I really don't know what to think, or what to make of her apology. It is definitely the last thing I expected. I have always tried to be a good person and not hold things against others, but that doesn't mean I forget. I would be a fool to do that. But I do try to take in the lessons learned and move on.

Still, I don't trust Molly.

I have a good life, full of love and laughter, and a husband that I adore. I have been very blessed. The least I can do is give her another chance. Withholding forgiveness is not my right.

"I accept yer apology," I finally say. The tears that immediately fill her green eyes soften me a little.

"Thank you," she says with a smile, wiping her face. "I appreciate yer kindness and I willna bother you again." As she walks to her car, she turns and calls, "You have a good day."

"You too."

Closing the door, I stand by the window and watch her drive away. A second later, Tavish's arms come around me.

"Are ye all right, love?"

"Truthfully, I don't know."

"It may be wrong of me, but I dinna trust her."

"I hate to admit it, but I feel the same."

* * *

Later in the night, I lay in the dark, wrapped in the haven of Tavish's arms, both of us boneless and sated from making love. I don't think there have ever been two bodies so perfectly made of one another. Our mutual desire is always there, burning beneath the surface, and the wanting never stops. The combination of his heated kisses, his caressing hands and his body wrapped around mine make me incoherent to the world around me and I can't even think. Sometimes all he has to do is look at me with those intent blue eyes and I melt. I am thankful every day to be his wife, to have him as my husband. He is mine. We belong to each other.

He is mine!

Sighing, my thoughts drift wayward and my mind roams to Molly's unexpected visit and apology. Tavish said he still doesn't trust her, convinced that she must be up to something, and I agree with him. I forgave her, yes, but I plan to be on my guard.

All my life I have had to fight my way through this world. My sisters have always been aggressive when it comes to getting what they want, and as a child I had to fight for my share of everything. I even had to fight for my mother's love. In school had to fight to not be overlooked. In the writing world I've had to fight to make my voice heard. Yes, I am used to fighting my way through life.

And I will fight for my husband with everything I have. No one will come between us.

"What are ye thinking about, my own?" His arms are draped about me, his hands caressing, his lips against my brow.

"About how much I love you, how happy you've made me, and how glad I am that you are mine."

"I *am* yers. I love ye more than me own life. You and no one else. And I'll love ye til my dying breath and beyond. I'll never stop." He moves back a little and presses a hand to my face, his fingers traveling over my cheeks and lips as his eyes find mine in the moonlight filling the room. "Your touch is life ta me. I wish I could lose myself in ye, hold you close to my heart and never part from ye or be without your hands on me in some way. I long ta worship yer mouth with mine every moment of the day, to crush you to me and become a part of you. Sometimes I fear I will burn up with need for ye. It never stops."

Tears filling my eyes, I press my trembling lips to his. To be loved so deeply and completely is more than I could ever ask for. "You are everything ta me," I whisper against his mouth as embers of the inferno that is our love rekindle.

Hungrily, he again takes me to the place that is ours alone, a place where powerful passion resides, making me forget, if only for a while, the threat that a part of me knows is still out there waiting to intrude upon our world.

Fourteen

Tavish and I share a mutual smile as we examine the test stick.

"Are you ready for this?" I ask him.

His gentle eyes roam over my face. "Aye. Are you?"

Being thirty-five and having wondered if childbearing would pass me by without experiencing motherhood makes it easy to answer, "Aye, I'm ready."

I have been sick on and off this past week and this morning was the worst so far. Having missed a period last month, it never dawned on me that I might be pregnant. Knowing for sure is a little overwhelming, but I couldn't be happier about it.

"I think your da is going ta dance a jig."

Tavish laughs, pulling me close and kissing my cheek. "I think ye're right. When do you want ta break the news?"

"Whenever you want is fine."

"Maybe I'll ring him now."

While he is on the phone with his father, I sift through today's mail, surprised, no, shocked to see a letter from my sister, Audrey. I haven't heard from Audrey or Yvonne since coming to Scotland and I can't help wondering if some thing is wrong. I hope everyone is okay and no one is sick or anything. Opening the envelope, I unfold the stationary.

Dear Adia,

Thank you from all of us for the announcement and congratulations. I also want to apologize for not replying or writing sooner. I still don't understand what made you decide to just pick up and move to Scotland, but I am glad for the turn your life took and I truly wish you every happiness.

We are doing okay here. Mama was sick for a

bit, but she is doing better. Since receiving your announcement, she seems to have found a renewed hope in life, and your marriage has given her something positive to latch on to. For Yvonne and I as well.

I know we haven't been the best sisters to you. We are truly sorry about that. We can't do anything about the past, be we can try to be better now. I am only sorry about all the wasted time. Believe it or not, we do love you. Very much.

Call when you can and tell us about your husband and your life there.

Take care.

Audrey

Wow! Talk about miracles!

I grab a box of tissues from the dresser. Tavish walks in just as I am drying my face.

"What's wrong, *mo ghraidh*?"

"Nothing. Something good, really. Unexpected but good."

I give him the letter to read. When he is done, he holds me, rocking me a little. "'Tis a wonderful letter. What time is it there?"

I think a moment. "It's about eight in the

evening. Yesterday." I smile and he chuckles.

"We'll ring them now."

* * *

And we do.

I hadn't realized just how much I have missed hearing their voices. No, we never talked much even when I was there. Maybe that is why I've missed them so much. With Mama, Audrey and Yvonne on the speaker phone, we catch up on everything. Mama does sound happier. She tells me how proud of me she is and my sisters say how happy they are for me. I soon give the phone to Tavish and he talks with them for a few minutes, telling them of his love for me. I even let him give them the news of my pregnancy. I can easily hear their excited shouts of congratulations. When he finally hands the phone back to me, they gush over Tavish's 'sexy' accent and comment on my slight one.

We talk for a few minutes more, then say goodbye with the promise to keep in touch.

* * *

Tonight Tavish takes me to dinner at *The George* to celebrate my pregnancy and the reconciliation with my family. I order the baked stuffed peppers with wild mushrooms and asparagus, he orders the grilled gammon steak and we share meals. I love the atmosphere, the wood decor, the flagstone floors, and the roaring log and peat fire we are seated near. The area is cozy and homey, and I always enjoy coming here.

"So when do ye think the baby is due?" Tavish asks me. We have finished our meal and are waiting to pay the check.

"According to the date calculation chart I looked up today, I am six weeks along and due in October."

Tavish's eyes drop to my flat stomach and he smiles, pressing a hand against me. "To have you carrying a part o me inside ye . . . 'tis a grand feeling."

"Aye, it is." I squeeze his hand. "And you will be an amazing father."

"I hope so. You will be a verra fine mother."

"I hope so too. And I know women my age have babies all the time, but I still worry a little. I'm pretty healthy, so hopefully there willna be any problems."

"Everything will be fine. Two of my nieces were delivered by a midwife here in Inveraray. Or would you feel more comfortable with a doctor?"

"I would kind of like to go the midwife route. I've heard great things about home births."

"Oh, aye. My sister Miriam birthed in the water and swears by it."

"Really? I'll have to talk with her about it."

"She'll be glad ta share, I'm sure."

While Tavish pays the check, I make a restroom visit. When I return to the table, he helps me into my coat and takes my hand. On our way to the door, we pass Molly who is dining alone. Her plate is empty and she is sipping coffee.

"How are ye this evening?" she asks.

Because I know Tavish won't answer, I do. "We're fine, and you?"

"I'm good. Thanks for asking."

It is an awkward moment, so I nod a goodbye and Tavish leads me away. As we exit the restaurant, he mumbles, "I still dinna trust her."

Fifteen

Molly

Molly has barely finished dressing when there is a hard knock on her room door.

"Who is it?"

"It's me."

The familiar sound of her co-worker's voice makes her heart pound. This is not good. His presence can only mean one thing. Her time is up. She opens the door and he strolls in. "What are ye doing here, Ben?"

He smiles, his dark eyes sparkling. "I'm here to see that things are done, since you can't seem to follow through."

"I've got it under control."

"Doesn't look like it. In fact, the boss thinks you're growing soft."

"I'm not."

"Then prove it. Since there's no chance of breaking them up now, we need to break *her*."

Molly's eyes narrow. "What do you mean?"

His bushy brows raise into his hairline. "Just what I said. It's payback time."

Grasping his meaning, Molly closes her eyes and shakes her head, done with the whole thing and fully aware of the consequences. Not only will she lose her job, but she could face jail time for skimming money for the boss. Of course, that she'd done it for him won't matter. He knows how to keep his hands clean. He can make a person see anything he wants. She supposes that's how she ended up falling in love with him in the first place. He made her see something that didn't exist, made her believe he actually had a heart. Oh, she will pay for this, but she doesn't care. Not anymore.

"I'm done."

He smirks, scratching his protruding belly

hanging over his belt buckle. "Yeah, I figured as much." He turns away for a moment, then suddenly his hand snaps out and the back of his fist lands against her eye. She staggers back and he grabs her hair, yanking her forward. She whimpers and he moves his face close to hers.

"Today we finish this. And I do mean *we*."

Sixteen

This morning Tavish left for Edinburgh to make a kilt delivery and pick up some supplies. Normally, I enjoy going on the drive with him, but the nausea that usually rears its head when I am in the car for long periods makes me bow out of this trip. I decide to spend the time reading instead.

> *"My love is like a red, red rose*
> *That's newly sprung in June:*
> *My love is like the melody*
> *That's sweetly played in tune.*
>
> *How fair art thou, my bonnie lass,*
> *So deep in love am I;*
> *And I will love thee still, my dear,*

Till all the seas gang dry.

Till all the seas gang dry, my dear,
And the rocks melt with the sun;
I will love thee still, my dear,
While the sands of life shall run.

And fare thee weel, my only love.
And fare thee weel awhile!
And I will come again, my love,
Though it were ten thousand mile."

Robert Burns is now my favorite poet. Tavish quotes his work to me frequently and says that he loves the plainly written emotion in them. I totally agree with him. He took me to the Burns Supper last month and it was one of the most enjoyable things I've ever done. An annual dinner held in honor of Scotland's most famous poet, lovers of his work usually meet on or around his birthday to celebrate his life. I had been so excited about attending, I wrote the whole itinerary down in my notebook so I wouldn't forget anything. Who knows, I might use the experience in a novel one day. Taking the notebook from the bookshelf, I read over what I wrote.

First: The host gives a welcoming speech.

Second: The guests gather and mingle and skim

*through Burns' work, some indulge in the whiskey selection,
and then we hear opening remarks.*

Third: Grace is said using the Selkirk Grace:

> **Some hae meat and canna eat,**
> **And some wad eat that want it;**
> **But we hae meat, and we can eat,**
> **And sae let the Lord be thankit.**

The supper is then started with a Scottish broth soup.

*Fourth: A piper plays the pipes and everyone stands
while the main course of haggis is brought in. Haggis is a
surprisingly delicious pudding containing sheep's heart,
liver and lungs, minced with onion, oatmeal, spices, and salt.
It's then mixed with meat stock and encased in the animal's
stomach or sausage casing.*

*Fifth: Someone recites the Address to a Haggis. (Note
to self: Too long to write even if I could remember it all, but
will Google it.)*

*Sixth: They have an Immortal Memory where one of
the guests gives a short speech, remembering something
about Burns' life or poetry.*

Seventh: The host says a few words of thanks.

*Eighth: Toast to the Lassies: A short speech is given
by a male guest, giving his amusing but non-offensive view
on women. The men then drink a toast to the health of the*

women.

Ninth: Reply from the Lassies: A female guest then shares her amusing views on men and replies to anything specific brought up by the previous speaker during his toast.

Tenth: Singing of Burns' Works and Closing: Some of Burns' songs are sung and the host calls on one of the guests to give the vote of thanks. Afterward, everyone stands, joins hands and sings Auld Lang Syne. *Then it ends.*

Closing the notebook, I chuckle, remembering how many people *couldn't* stand for the closing due to a little too much whiskey toasting. I think Tavish and I were the only sober people there. We were high on each other, drunk on love.

Warmth spreads through me as I remember that night. We came home and Tavish softly quoted Burns while we made love. I am definitely married to the most romantic man in the world.

Sighing, I put the notebook back on the shelf and head down to the kitchen to decide on what to fix for dinner. So far, I can still stomach my favorite meals, and since I've read that it will not always be the case, I'm enjoying everything while still I can.

Just as I enter the kitchen, something hard

crashes against my head. There is a second of blinding pain, then I feel no more.

Seventeen

Slowly awakening, I wince. I am cold and my head aches beyond description. Prying my eyes open, it takes my vision a moment to adjust. I am outside somewhere. The woods. That's where I am, somewhere in the woods. And night has fallen.

But where? How did I get here? Who did this? How long have I been here? The cold stiffness clutching my body and the dark skies answer the latter question. As for who, there can only be one answer.

Molly.

Managing to sit up a moment, I attempt to stand,

but the sharp pain shooting up my leg makes it impossible and I fall over. Looking at my feet, I gasp. My left foot is turned at an odd angle, the top bent over. There is no question that it is broken. Badly broken. *She broke my foot so I couldn't walk back, maybe hoping I will freeze to death. But she couldn't have done this alone . . .*

Shivering, I huddle against a pine tree and wrap my arms around my middle, longing for the smallest bit of warmth. I was left with no coat and I am only wearing a light sweater and a skirt with no socks or shoes. I never wear shoes around the house, just socks or I go barefoot. Every part of my body is freezing, including the tears that lie frozen on my cheeks. I can't really see anything, but I am so lost, having light wouldn't matter anyway. I wouldn't be able to walk if I *could* see. Trying not to lose hope is wearing me down, and I am so tired I can't think anymore, the cold is fogging my brain.

Still, as my eyes begin losing their fight to remain open, I murmur one phrase over and over as they finally slip shut.

"Please find me, Tavish. God, please help him

find me. Please . . ."

* * *

When I next awaken, it is still dark, but I am warm. An unfamiliar scent surrounds me, the smell of something wild. My eyes slip shut again, my mind and body too exhausted to think, or care anymore.

* * *

Tavish

For the first time in his life, Tavish MacLachlan is entertaining thoughts of murder. He wants to kill with his bare hands, but the person he wants to inflict this pain on is no longer around. However, the man managed to leave brutality in his wake. Now, wandering in the dark, all Tavish can think about is finding his wife. His mind mercilessly goes over today's events again.

When Tavish had gotten home and found Adia gone, then spotted the broken vase on the floor lying amid drops of blood, something inside him snapped. He had rushed through the house yelling Adia's name, then he'd searched the yard. He immediately called Evan and Ian, two friends who are also policemen. They told him to wait there, but he couldn't. All he could think about was her lying somewhere freezing to death.

Bolting to the car, he had one intended destination: The Inverary Hotel. He was prepared to break Molly's room door down, but before he could back out of the driveway, Molly pulled up. He watched her get out of her car, sucking in a breath when he saw her face. One of her eyes was swollen shut, her lips and nose bleeding. Someone had gotten her good. However, there was no time for sympathy.

"Where is she?" Tavish's gravelly voice was like ice.

"I don't know. He came to my hotel room this morning and forced me ta bring him here. He knocked Adia out and took her."

"Who is he?"

"A coworker from the states."

Tavish stalked toward Molly and she backed up a bit. "Ye're going ta tell me everything and ye're going ta tell me quickly." At that moment, Evan and Ian pulled up. Tavish waited until the two men had joined them. "Dinna leave anything out."

Shivering from both fear and the cold, Molly

spilled the whole story.

"I have been working for a publisher in New York . . . the same publisher Adia was under contract with. We had never met, but I knew who she was."

Every part of Tavish was suddenly strung as tight as a bow. "Go on," he growled and she quickly continued.

"A few weeks after Adia left, the boss'–Tom Leader is his name–his wife received an anonymous letter detailing his sexual advances toward Adia, as well as the other women in the office. He said Adia did it ta ruin him and she wouldna get away with it. His wife is now taking him for everything, including the company. It became his goal to get back at Adia."

Molly wiped the tears streaking her face. "He called one of her sisters and asked about her. He was told that she'd moved here. I'm . . . ashamed ta admit that I was . . . sleeping with Tom and he knew everythin' about me, including where I was from. When I told him I used to live in Inveraray, he immediately booked a flight for me and gave me instructions. I was told ta make Adia's life hell, to hurt her physically if necessary. But I couldna physically harm her. I just couldn't. My job was on the line. And since I hadn't accomplished what I was sent here ta do, he sent another ruthless employee to help. I didn't want to be a part of it anymore, but he didn't agree. I tried ta stop him from taking Adia, but . . . I couldn't."

Tavish was literally shaking, a mixture of anger and fear surging through him. Never laying a hand on a woman before, he wanted to grip Molly's neck and shake her until he got all the information he could, but he was saved from asking any more questions when Evan and Ian took over.

"What is the man's name?" Evan asked.

"Ben Thurgood. He's a glorified errand boy at the office."

"And where is he now?"

"I don' know. I havena seen him since. I think I lost consciousness for a bit because when I came to, he was gone."

"Why didn't ye come ta the station?" Ian asked.

"I don't know. I was afraid, I guess."

Tavish tugged a hand back through his hair, impatient to begin searching. "What did he say he planned ta do with her?"

Molly's voice broke. "He was . . . he was going ta dump her somewhere."

Drawing his thoughts to the present, Tavish, Evan and Ian comb yet another forest area, the beams from their flashlights illuminating their surroundings. His emotions scream to be released, but he knows he must keep it together. He has to until he finds Adia. It is bitter cold and his pregnant wife is somewhere suffering. The thought of this is more than he can bear. She is everything to him and if he lost her, he would die too.

It is beginning to snow now and the men spread out again to cover more ground. Tavish quickens his pace. "Please, God," he murmurs. "Please help me find her."

Just ahead of him something moves in the trees. He stops and shines his light into the area, completely startled when a large doe walks out. She stands still for a moment, just looking at him and he stares back. Then she slowly turns back the way she came, stopping and looking back at him again. Puzzled, Tavish's brow furrows. She is still standing there, almost like she is waiting for him to follow.

"Is that it?" he softly asks. "Are ye waiting for me, girl?" She starts walking again and Tavish follows, shining the light as he moves through the trees, fighting his way through limbs and branches. The doe walks ahead and after a few minutes, she stops.

"What is it, girl?" Tavish reaches the animal and she moves aside, exposing a small mound, then she runs off. He drops to his knees.

"Oh, Adia."

Eighteen

"Tavish?"

"I'm here, *mo ghraidh.*"

I try to open my eyes, but the light is blinding and hurts too much, so I keep them closed. There is no pain now, and the sound of my husband's beloved voice and the warmth of his hand holding mine is comforting.

"Thirsty," I struggle to say. My throat is dry, making it hard to talk.

He releases my hand and a moment later says, "Here's some water, darlin'," pressing a straw to my lips. I take a few sips and thank him. Again, I attempt to open my eyes, and after several times, they slowly adjust. "Where am I?"

"Hospital, in Glasgow."

"So glad you found me."

Tavish doesn't say anything and I try to focus in on his features. When they become clear, I'm shocked by what I see. His hair is disheveled, his face unshaven, his eyes tired, and it occurs to me that I must have been in bad shape when they found me.

"How long have I been here?"

Tavish squeezes my hand, his face a tired mask. "Two days."

"Two days?" I unconsciously move my free hand to my stomach, afraid to ask but needing to know. "The baby?"

"The baby is fine, love. Just fine."

Remembering my foot, I glance down the bed, noticing the mound of my right foot sticking up under the covers, but not the left. Tears filling my eyes, I raise my gaze to his. "No," I whisper.

"I'm so sorry. They tried . . . but they couldna save it. 'Twas too damaged. I'm so sorry."

Sitting on the bed, Tavish wraps me in his arms and I cry. I cry for the loss of my foot, for the anguish he has gone through, and for the terrible situation I've brought into his life. Then the tears become ones of gratitude. How thankful I am that Tavish found me, that our baby is okay, and that I am alive. The loss of my foot is great, but that loss is far outweighed by the blessings.

Wiping away the last of the tears, I take a deep breath and concentrate on the fact that I am still here. This is what matters. I do still wonder, though, exactly what happened.

"Tavish?"

"Hmmm?"

His answer rumbles against my ear like the purr of a big cat and I smile. "Tell me everything. What happened?"

"Later, darlin'."

"No, now. Please."

Burying his face in my hair, he inhales and releases a deep sigh. "All right, my own. I will tell ye everything."

Tavish shares the entire unbelievable tale. When

he finishes, I honestly don't know what to think. To know Molly tried to stop what happened to me is a small relief, but that Tom Leader could even be behind this and sanction something so cruel just blows my mind. I never saw Molly at the New York office, but I do remember seeing Ben Thurgood a couple of times in passing. He never seemed that friendly.

"And he got away?"

"Aye," he sighs. "But put yer mind at ease. He willna ever come here again. I hate that he got away with what he did, but Evan and Ian will do what they can ta insure he doesna step foot on Scotland's shores again."

I nod, grateful for the men and their friendship. Next to Tavish and his father, there aren't two finer men in Inveraray. "And Molly?" I can't help feeling a bit sorry for her.

"Going to London ta live with her parents. She isna returning to the states. She says she's starting over. 'Tis fitting, I think."

"It is." Despite what she did, I hope things work out for her and she can find happiness, and though I will never forget, I do forgive her. I have so much to be grateful for, I won't waste a moment being bitter.

I silently thank God again for helping Tavish find me. What a miracle that was! I am still amazed by what he told me. To think, a doe kept me warm, and that same doe led him to me. It's incredible. I was truly being watched over, and that is a knowledge I will always treasure.

Squeezing his hand, I take in his indiscernible expression and ask, "How are you? I know this hasn't been easy for you."

He smiles, his bottom lip trembling slightly. "I'll be fine."

I know he has been holding himself together for me. I also know he needs me. "When can I go home?"

"Now that ye're awake, hopefully in a few days."

My eyes move to my missing foot again briefly. "I love you, Tavish. And I will try not to be a burden."

"I love you, *mo chridhe*. You could never be a burden. Dinna ever think it."

Nineteen

Two days later

It is so good to be home. The doctor sent me off with crutches, and after testing them up and down the hospital halls a few times, I have adjusted. Once the stub has healed, I can wear a prosthetic foot, and other than a slight limp, I'll be able to walk normally. I consider this a major blessing.

While I was in the hospital, Tavish had someone come in and clean up the broken vase and the blood. Thinking about it, I gingerly touch the back of my head. The wound hadn't needed many stitches, though it is still a little sore. I'll have to be careful when doing my hair, so a ponytail will work for a while.

Tavish takes the crutches from me and carries me up to our room. Since we have a sitting area there with a small sofa and television, as well as a mini fridge in my office, there is no need for me to go back down today. Tavish has made sure I have everything I need. We know I can't stay up here forever, but today I will accept his pampering.

He gently places me on the bed and gets a pain pill for me. Taking his hand, I pull him down beside me. Saying nothing, he simply pulls the extra quilt over us and gathers me in his arms, holding me close. My head is against his chest and his heart is pounding against my ear, the mad rhythm startling. I ask him if he is all right, but instead of answering, he holds me tighter against him.

Then the shaking begins. One by one the shudders rip through him and he begins to sob. Tightening my embrace, I cry with him. This is why he'd kept his emotions locked away. If he had allowed them to surface, he wouldn't have been able to rein them in. He had done it for me, and now it is my turn to comfort him.

Wiping his tears with my fingers, I press my mouth to his, and his response is automatic and voracious, the passion between us immediate and unbridled. With my lips and hands, I attempt to take his pain away, absorbing as much as I possibly can. His words are in Gaelic. Some I understand, some I don't, but the familiar *mo ghraidh* and *mo chridhe*–my love and my heart–come through clearly. Emotions grow more intense, and when we finally become one, there are no more words.

Outside our home, the world goes on without us, nothing changed by the events that have happened. But here, in our own little world, everything has changed, our life altered in ways we could never have imagined. For this moment, we create our own oblivion and wrap ourselves in it.

As I lay in Tavish's arms afterward and begin to drift with his murmured "I love you" in my ear, I understand now that though my body may no longer be perfect, the life, and love I've been blessed with are perfect for me. I know everything will be okay. *I* will be okay.

On the edge of sleep, the last paragraph of my grandmother's journal comes to mind, most likely because it was written specifically for me, and it is fitting.

I finally decided that no matter what trials came my way, I would roll with them and work through them. Then I would take control and become stronger. Adversity is a part of life, and trials are meant to teach, mold and shape each of us into the person we were meant to be all along. Only after coming through the refiner's fire will our true selves shine through.

Remember this and be grateful, Adia. Always be grateful.

Excerpt from

$\mathcal{I}$f $\mathcal{Y}$ou're $\mathcal{N}$ot the $\mathcal{O}$ne

Book Two of the Highland Romance Trilogy

Inveraray Scotland

Drawing strength from Tavish's comforting embrace, I dry my face. I just spent the last hour on the phone with Audrey, crying empathetic tears, sharing her sorrow. Her news had been bitter-sweet, but the time for tears has passed and now it's time for action.

"We should get the guest room ready," Tavish murmurs against my brow. "'Twill be a difficult transition for yer sister."

I nod. "Are you really okay with this?"

"Aye. She's family. And we have the room. Question is, are *you* all right with everythin'?"

"Aye," I answer back. "I want ta do everything I can ta help her. She needs a new beginning and Inveraray is the perfect place. 'Twas for me. Hopefully she can find the happiness she deserves."

* * *

Salt Lake City, Utah

Audrey Stone is an emotional wreck.

Two months ago, in a moment of loneliness, she made the dumbest decision of her life, and the consequence of that choice is major. She has no excuse. She had been at a low point when she ran into her ex, and had willingly given in to his desires. The next day he was gone.

Now Audrey is pregnant and the baby will never know the father.

Pulling a couple of suitcases from the hall closet, Audrey begins to pack. She hates intruding upon her sister's life, but the offer to have her come and stay with them was just what she needed. She is excited about starting over somewhere new and is looking forward to seeing Adia again, as well as meeting her husband, but she won't wear out her welcome. She will stay with them just until she can settle into a new life there.

Because now there is more than just herself to think about.

About the Author

    J. (Jewel) Adams stays crazy busy with her family and writing. She has written several books in different

genres and is also a motivational speaker to both youthand adult audiences.

In her spare time (when she has any) she likes to curl up with a good book and a healthy stash of orange Tic Tacs. She and her family reside in Utah.

Jewel loves hearing from her fans. You can contact her at jewela40@gmail.com

Blogs:

jewelsbestgems.blogspot.com
my-beauty-personifies.blogspot.com

Websites:
JewelAdams.com
thehighlandtrilogy.weebly.com

www.ingramcontent.com/pod-product-compliance
Lightning Source LLC
Chambersburg PA
CBHW071304130626

46556CB00003B/1463